Level 4 is ideal for children who are ready to ████ ████ ███ with a wider
vocabulary and are eager to start reading in █████

Special features:

Full,
citing story

Heidi was happy in the mountains
with her grandfather. She liked
the trees and flowers and she liked
looking after the goats with Peter.
Heidi liked the little white goat best of
all. Her name was Snowflake.

15

14

Clear type

Richer, more
varied vocabulary

Heidi was pleased to see Clara, and
took her to see all the beautiful things
in the mountains.

But Peter was jealous of Heidi's new
friend. When no one was looking,
he pushed Clara's wheelchair down
the mountain.

Longer sentences

Detailed illustrations
to capture
the imagination

40

41

Educational Consultant: Geraldine Taylor

A catalogue record for this book is available from the British Library

Published by Ladybird Books Ltd
80 Strand, London, WC2R 0RL
A Penguin Company

001 - 10 9 8 7 6 5 4 3 2 1
© LADYBIRD BOOKS LTD MMXI
Ladybird, Read It Yourself and the Ladybird Logo are registered or
unregistered trade marks of Ladybird Books Limited.

ISBN: 978-1-40930-718-1

Printed in China

Heidi

Illustrated by Tamsin Hinrichsen

Once upon a time, there was a little girl called Heidi.

Heidi lived in a little town in Switzerland with her Aunt Dete. The town was near some mountains.

One day, Aunt Dete said, "Today we will go and see your grandfather. He lives up in the mountains."

As they walked up into the mountains, they saw a boy called Peter. Peter looked after some mountain goats.

Heidi and Aunt Dete walked up to the house where Grandfather lived. Grandfather came out to meet them.

9

Aunt Dete said, "Heidi, I have to go to Frankfurt. You must stay here with your grandfather."

Heidi was worried. So was her grandfather. He said, "I'm much too old to look after a little girl."

11

But Aunt Dete went back down the mountain, and Heidi stayed with her grandfather.

"Where will I sleep?" she asked.

Grandfather made her a little bed in the hayloft. Then Peter took Heidi some goat's milk to drink.

Heidi was happy in the mountains with her grandfather. She liked the trees and flowers and she liked looking after the goats with Peter. Heidi liked the little white goat best of all. Her name was Snowflake.

15

Sometimes, Heidi went to see Peter's grandma, who was blind. Heidi told Peter's grandma about all the beautiful trees and flowers that she saw in the mountains.

But one day, Aunt Dete came back from Frankfurt.

"Heidi," she said, "it's time you went to school."

"Where must I go?" said Heidi.

"To Frankfurt," said Aunt Dete, "I will take you to stay with my friends who live there."

Grandfather was sad. "Does Heidi have to go?" he said.

Heidi was sad, too. "I want to stay here with Grandfather and Peter," she said.

But Aunt Dete said, "No. You must go to school."

Aunt Dete took Heidi to live with some of her friends in a big house in Frankfurt.

A little girl called Clara lived there. Clara could not walk. She had to stay in a wheelchair all the time.

Heidi liked Clara, but she wasn't happy living in Frankfurt. She wanted to go back to Grandfather and Peter in the mountains.

At night, Heidi dreamed that she was in the mountains with Snowflake, the little white goat.

One day, when Heidi came home from school, Clara said, "Last night, the maid saw a ghost on the stairs. Tonight, Daddy will stay up so that he can see the ghost, too."

So that night, Clara's father went to look for the ghost. His friend, the doctor, went with him. As they were looking, there was a noise on the stairs. It was Heidi, walking in her sleep.

"So this is the ghost, after all," said Clara's father.

The doctor took Heidi back to her bedroom.

"What were you dreaming about?" said the doctor.

"I was dreaming of the mountains," said Heidi. "I am happy here, but I miss my grandfather and Peter."

31

Clara's father was worried about Heidi. "I'll help you to go home," he said.

Heidi went to see Clara. "I will miss you when I am back in the mountains," she said.

"I will miss you, too," said Clara. "But I will come and see you one day soon."

So Heidi went back to the mountains. Grandfather and Peter were very happy to see her. Peter gave her some goat's milk. Then Heidi went to sleep in the hayloft.

Heidi didn't walk in her sleep that night. She was so happy to be home.

The next day, Heidi went to look after the goats with Peter.

"It's wonderful to have you back," said Peter. "I missed you."

"I missed you, too," said Heidi. "I want to stay in the mountains for ever."

One morning, when Heidi had just got up, there was a knock at the door. It was Clara and her father.

"I have to go to town," said Clara's father. "Clara can stay here with you for a week."

Heidi was pleased to see Clara, and took her to see all the beautiful things in the mountains.

But Peter was jealous of Heidi's new friend. When no one was looking, he pushed Clara's wheelchair down the mountain.

The next day, Clara could not find her wheelchair.

"I must try to walk," said Clara. So Heidi and her grandfather helped her to walk.

Suddenly, Clara started to walk all by herself. "This is wonderful!" said Heidi.

Peter was pleased, too. "I'm so sorry I was jealous," said Peter. "Will you be my friend, Clara?"

The next day, Clara's father came to take her back home. Clara walked out of the house to meet him.

"You can walk!" said Clara's father. "This is the happiest day of my life."

And Heidi, Clara and Peter were friends for ever.

How much do you remember about the story of Heidi? Answer these questions and find out!

- Who did Heidi live with in the town in Switzerland?

- Who looked after the goats in the mountains?

- What was the name of Heidi's favourite little white goat?

- Why did Heidi have to go to Frankfurt?

- What did Peter do to Clara's wheelchair?

- Why was Clara's father surprised at the end?

Look at these words. Unjumble them to make words from the story and match them to the pictures.

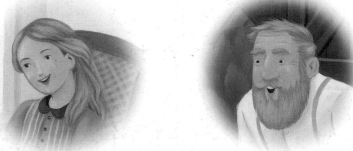

tomianuns

Hiied

natherdfarg

Preet

Swonlakfe

Craal

Read it yourself
with Ladybird

Read it yourself — with Ladybird — Level 1 — The Three Billy Goats Gruff

Read it yourself — with Ladybird — Level 1 — Cinderella

Read it yourself — with Ladybird — Level 1 — Little Red Hen

Read it yourself — with Ladybird — Level 1 — Goldilocks and the Three Bears

Read it yourself — with Ladybird — Level 1 — The Enormous Turnip

Read it yourself — with Ladybird — Level 1 — The Magic Porridge Pot

Read it yourself — with Ladybird — Level 1 — The Ugly Duckling

Read it yourself — with Ladybird — Level 2 — The Gingerbread Man

Read it yourself — with Ladybird — Level 2 — Sleeping Beauty

Read it yourself — with Ladybird — Level 2 — Little Red Riding Hood

Read it yourself — with Ladybird — Level 2 — Sly Fox and Red Hen

Read it yourself — with Ladybird — Level 2 — The Three Little Pigs

Read it yourself — with Ladybird — Level 2 — Town Mouse and Country Mouse

Read it yourself — with Ladybird — Level 2 — Chicken Licken

Read it yourself — with Ladybird — Level 3 — The Elves and the Shoemaker

Read it yourself — with Ladybird — Level 3 — Jack and the Beanstalk

Read it yourself — with Ladybird — Level 3 — Hansel and Gretel

Read it yourself — with Ladybird — Level 4 — The Pied Piper of Hamelin

Read it yourself — with Ladybird — Level 4 — The Wizard of Oz

Read it yourself — with Ladybird — Level 4 — Heidi

Collect all the titles in the series.